A
Horse Named
Sage

MILTON HEILWEIL

To order additional copies of this book, contact:
Xlibris
844-714-8691
www.Xlibris.com
Orders@Xlibris.com

ISBN: Softcover   978-1-6698-0532-8
         Hardcover   978-1-6698-0533-5
         EBook   978-1-6698-0531-1

Print information available on the last page

Rev. date: 03/03/2022

A
Horse Named
Sage

Like my dad I loved horses and always dreamed of having my own horse.

For my 13th birthday my mom and dad surprised me with the greatest present I could ever get… a horse!

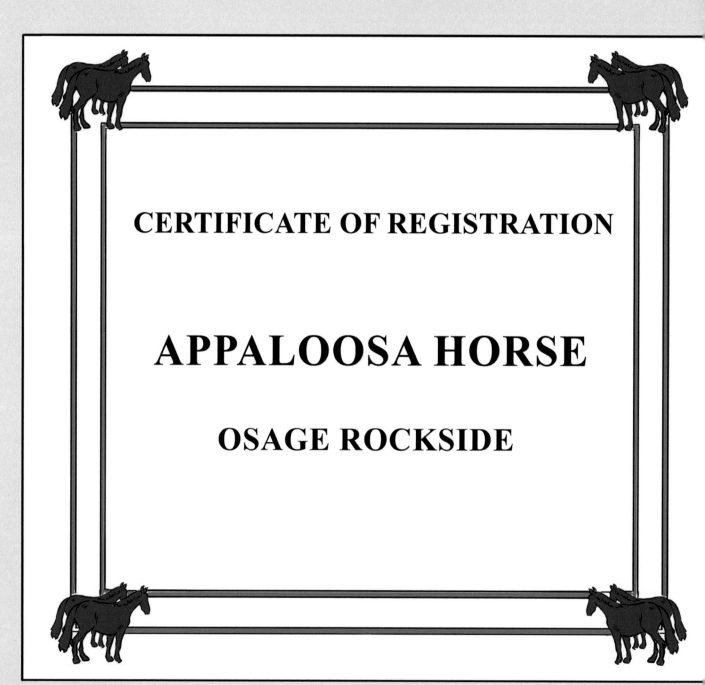

CERTIFICATE OF REGISTRATION

APPALOOSA HORSE

OSAGE ROCKSIDE

His registered name was Osage Rockside and we decided to call him "Sage"

Like me, Sage was 13 years old. He, like his mother (the mare) and his father (the stallion) were appaloosas.

The appaloosa (breed) was often the horse Native Americans liked because they are smart and could run fast.

It's easy to pick out an appaloosa horse. They all have dark spots on a white background. The rest of the horse could be brown or black. Sometime they are white with spots all over. Some with spots only on their backside (rump). That's called a blanket.

Sage was a handsome brown horse brown with a good looking blanket.

Sage was trained to be a cowboy's horse he could run fast and stop on a dime. Your wish was his command.

We had a big backyard and my dad had a barn built for Sage.

Sage liked his new home. I helped my dad to build a fence around the barn called a corral. Sage would run free in the corral and sometimes roll in the dirt to scratch his back.

Every morning before school. I would get up early (it was still dark) to bring Sage fresh water and bring him his breakfast, grain and hay.

Sage always liked a treat. Sometimes my mom would bring carrots and apples home for our dinner. I would take some and give them to Sage. Sage always got the best ones.

When I got home from school I would do my chores, clean Sage's stall and then covered his floor with fresh wood shavings, when I finished with his stall I would brush his coat and it would shine.

I joined our local 4-h. A group that helped kids to grow up to be good kids. On weekends I often rode Sage in 4-h shows. The shows were contests to see who could ride best and control their horse through the course.

Both Sage and I liked riding in shows. Sage was the best! Together we often won, getting many blue ribbons and trophies.

30

Sage taught me to always do the job right and be a responsible person. We grew up together. He lived a long, long time. Sage was a good friend.